THE EVERYTHING MACHINE

by Matt Novak

A NEAL PORTER BOOK
ROARING BROOK PRESS
NEW YORK

To Michael and Molly

Copyright © 2009 by Matt Novak

A Neal Porter Book

Published by Roaring Brook Press

Roaring Brook Press is a division of

Holtzbrinck Publishing Holdings Limited Partnership

175 Fifth Avenue, New York, New York 10010

All rights reserved

www.roaringbrookpress.com

Distributed in Canada by H. B. Fenn and Company, Ltd.

Cataloging-in-Publication Data is on file at the Library of Congress

ISBN-13: 978-1-59643-286-4

ISBN-10: 1-59643-286-1

Roaring Brook Press books are available for special promotions and premiums.

For details, contact: Director of Special Markets, Holtzbrinck Publishers.

Printed in China

First edition October 2009

2 4 6 8 10 9 7 5 3 1

Far away on the planet Quirk
there was an amazing machine.
It was called the "Everything Machine."

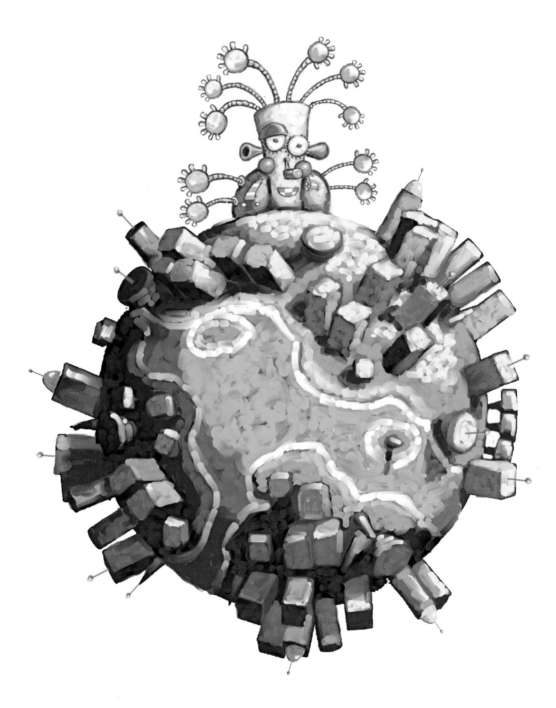

Every morning the loud *Chug! Chug!* of its engines awakened the people of Quirk, and every evening the soft *Puff! Puff!* of its smokestacks lulled them to sleep.

On most days, however, the Quirkians just stayed in bed.

No one had to do anything because the Everything Machine cleaned their houses, cooked their meals, mowed their lawns, and more.

It did all of those things they found difficult or boring.
It even colored their coloring books and scratched their backs.

It hadn't always been this way. Many, many years ago, long before anyone could remember, the planet Quirk was a very busy place.

Everyone worked hard to paint their houses

and grow their food.

Everything they needed they had to make themselves.

They were perfectly content until a visitor
from another planet landed on Quirk.
"Do you work too much?" he asked.
"Yes!" the Quirkians replied.

"Would you like your life to be more fulfilling?" the visitor asked.
"Yes!" the Quirkians answered.
"I have the solution to all of your problems," said the visitor.
The Quirkians were thrilled and shouted, "We'll take it! We'll take it!"

The visitor installed the Everything Machine and then flew away, never to be seen again.

Hundreds of years passed,

and the Quirkians came to rely on the machine more and more.

It painted their houses and grew their food.

Everything they needed the machine provided.
Eventually, they forgot what work was.

But one day, the machine just stopped.
There was no *Chug! Chug!* from the engines
and no *Puff! Puff!* from the smokestacks.

The anxious Quirkians gathered around the silent machine.
"My lawn needs to be mowed!" Mister Galaxia told the machine.
"Where is my breakfast?" moaned Miss Cosmosis.
"My coloring book needs to be colored," groaned Little Greebo Moonhead.
But the machine did nothing.

They tried to fix it.
They loosened nuts
and tightened bolts,
but that didn't work.

They talked softly
to it and caressed it
gently, but that
didn't work either.

They kicked it and
screamed, "Go! Go! Go!"
but nothing they did
could fix the machine.

Then someone discovered
a small label.

When machine is broken,
When machine goes wrong,
There's one thing to do:
Call Planet Bing Bong.

They called Planet Bing Bong, and a repairman flew right over.
He took the machine apart.

"This will take longer than I thought," he said, and went to work.

At first the Quirkians just stood around not knowing what to do.

Who will
mow my lawn?

Who will
make my breakfast?

Who will
color my books?

Soon they realized they had to learn how to do all those things and more.

It wasn't easy.

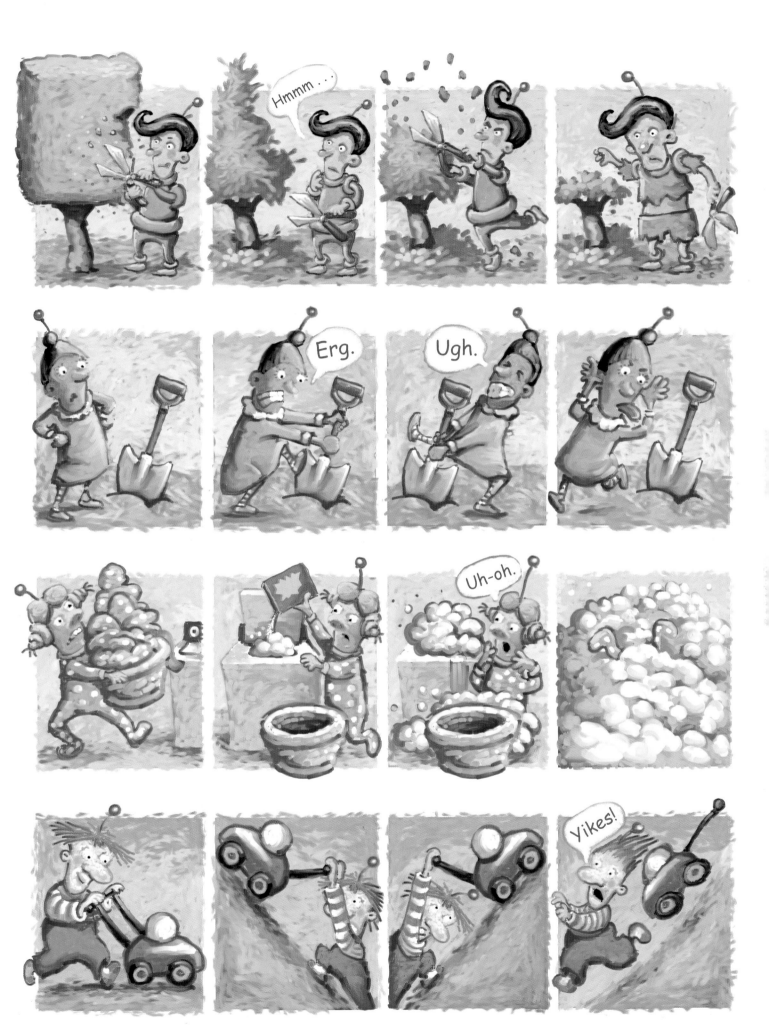

But slowly the cleaning, the cooking, the mowing,
and all those things the machine once did for them became easier.

Then it became fun.

"I really enjoy gardening," said Mister Galaxia. He gave Miss Cosmosis a bouquet of Quirk Carnations.

"Cooking is quite exhilarating," said Miss Cosmosis. She invited Mister Galaxia over for some Quirk casserole.

"I've finished my painting!" announced Little Greebo Moonhead. He proudly showed it to everyone.

It took months and months,
but finally the Everything Machine was fixed.
"It had a floobulated gromich," said the repairman,
holding up the broken part.

He flipped the switch.
The machine went into action.
"Hooray!" everyone cried. "Let's have a party!"

"I will make the food," said Miss Cosmosis, but the machine had already cooked it.

"I will make beautiful flower arrangements," said Mister Galaxia, but the machine had already arranged them.

"I will paint all the banners," said Little Greebo Moonhead, but the machine had already painted them.

Everything should have been as peaceful and relaxing as before, but it wasn't.

The next day the machine tried to water Mister Galaxia's Quirk Carnations. "Stay out of my garden!" he yelled.

It served Miss Cosmosis breakfast in bed. "I'll make my own omelets!" howled Miss Cosmosis.

The machine grabbed Little Greebo Moonhead's crayons and coloring book. "I want to do it myself!" shouted the boy.

The Everything Machine was just getting in the way now.
"I don't need a machine anymore," said Little Greebo, and everyone agreed.

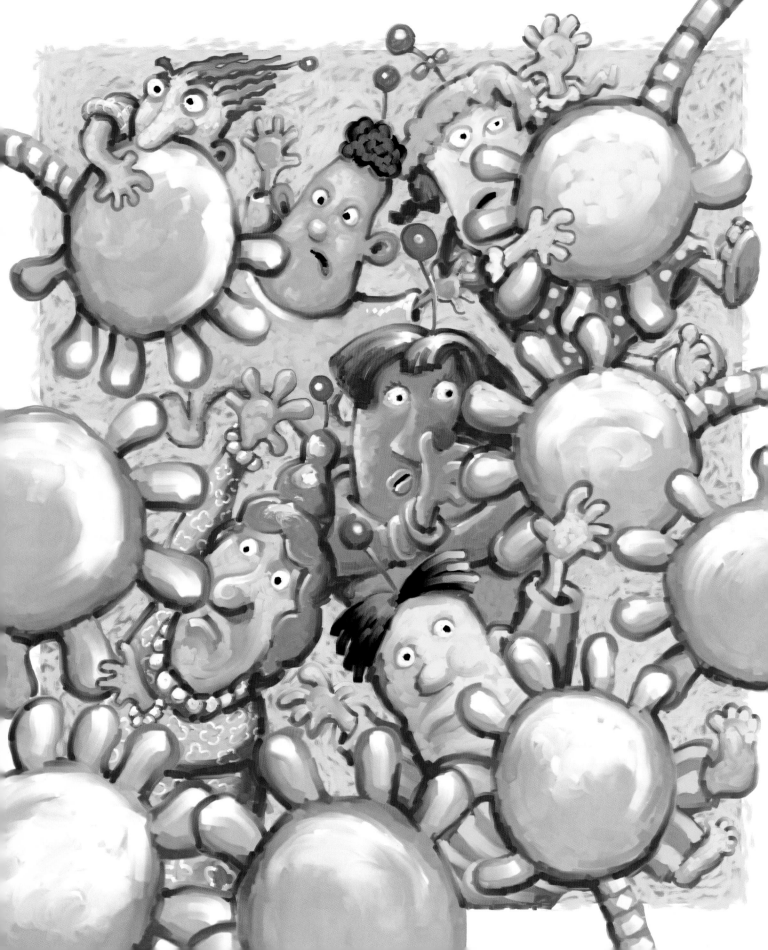

On Saturday they had a meeting.
"What should we do with it?" asked Mister Galaxia.
"I could dismantle it," said the repairman,
but the Quirkians did not like that idea.

"I do like the *Chug! Chug!*" said Miss Cosmosis.
"I have missed the *Puff! Puff!*" said Little Greebo Moonhead.
"It has been very good to us over the years," said Mister Galaxia.
Everyone agreed.

So they built a beautiful park around it.

The repairman made a few adjustments,
and, while the Quirkians went about their busy, happy, full days,

the machine was always there to do the one job
that is probably the most difficult of all . . .

. . . back scratching.

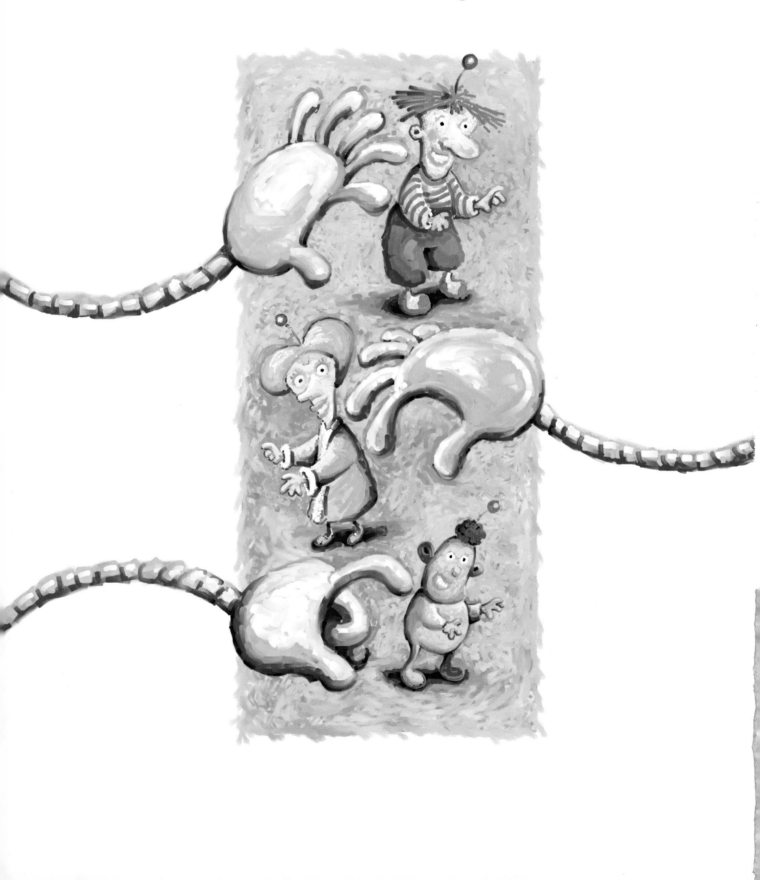